The MEGAMOGS

For Jack

First published 1994

3 5 7 9 10 8 6 4 2

Copyright © Peter Haswell 1994

*Peter Haswell has
asserted his right under the Copyright, Designs
and Patents Act, 1988 to be identified as the
author/illustrator of this work.*

*First publshed in the United Kingdom 1994 by
The Bodley Head Children's Books
Random House, 20 Vauxhall Bridge Road,
London SW1V 2SA*

*Random House Australia (Pty) Limited
20 Alfred Street, Milsons Point, Sydney,
New South Wales 2061, Australia*

*Random House New Zealand Limited
18 Poland Road, Glenfield,
Auckland 10, New Zealand*

*Random House South Africa (Pty) Limited
PO Box 337, Bergvlei 2012, South Africa*

Random House UK Limited Reg. No. 954009

*A CIP catalogue record for this book is
available from the British Library*

ISBN 0 370 31874 9

Printed in Singapore

THE MEGAMOGS

Peter Haswell

Glitzy Mitzy

Derek Dogbender

Kevin Catflap

Fishpaste Fred

Ginger Brownsauce

The Bodley Head
London

In a quaint little old house lived a quaint little old lady called Miss Marbletop. Miss Marbletop collected mogs. And she had a whole mighty, magnificent, mindless, moronic, mog-eared mob of them. They were called Miss Marbletop's Megamogs.

It was on Monday morning that Miss Marbletop went off in her old, red sports car.

It was on Monday afternoon that Kevin Catflap, Captain of the Megamogs, addressed the others.

'Right,' said Kevin Catflap. 'We're going to paint the house.'

'I vote we paint it pink,' said Tracy Tinopener.

'Green,' growled Fishpaste Fred.

'Puce,' piped up Phil Fleacollar.

'Red!' shouted Ginger Brownsauce and Gary Gristle.

'ORDER! ORDER!' cried Kevin Catflap. 'Never mind the colour – JUST PAINT!'

AND SO THE
MEGAMOGS PAINTED
MISS MARBLETOP'S
HOUSE

And this is how it looked.

'Great!' exclaimed Kevin Catflap. 'Nice paintwork. Now, I want everyone in bed early. Tomorrow we've got real work to do – so no going out on the tiles. No serenading or parading. No dustbin bashing, bottle smashing, rooting tooting alley-scooting, caterwauling, bawling or squalling. I want everybody up and awake, bright eyed and bushy tailed, ready to give it some welly tomorrow at seven. Right?'

'What's the job, Kev?' asked Barry Binliner.

'I'm not saying yet,' said Kevin, darkly. 'But it's going to be BIG!'

7.00 am Tuesday. The Megamogs put on their hard hats…

"HEIGH HO! HEIGH HO!"

Then they brought in diggers, dumpers, bulldozers, picks, shovels, cement mixers, cones, signs and…

They built a mighty highway
right past the front of
Miss Marbletop's house.

'Great!' pronounced Kevin Catflap. 'Nice highway. Now – early to bed and early to rise. No all nighting, fighting or moonlighting. No howling, yowling or prowling. I want you all here, up with the larks, whisker sharp and raring to go tomorrow at seven.'

'What's the plan, Kev?' asked Glitzy Mitzy.

'I'll give you a clue,' said Kevin. 'It's going to be BIG!'

Then they dug foundations, drove piles, brought in cranes, raised girders high into the sky, heaved, hauled, sweated, strained and built…

An enormous office block right behind Miss Marbletop's house.

'Great!' declared Kevin Catflap.
'Nice office block. Now – everyone
gets an early night. Right? No
partying, prancing and dancing.
No disco diving, go-go jiving, boogie
bopping, night-spot hopping. We've
got to be up and at 'em, on the ball
and tails tingling at sparrow squeak
tomorrow.'

'OK Kev,' said Derek Dogbender.
'What's the deal this time?'

'You'll see,' said Kevin Catflap.
'It's going to be BIG!'

7.00 am Thursday.
The Megamogs put on their workboots.

Then they humped, heaved, dragged, dug, drilled, moiled, toiled, boiled, huffed, puffed, grumbled, groused, growled, groaned, bellyached and built…

A huge airport behind the office block at the back of Miss Marbletop's house.

'Great!' grinned Kevin Catflap. 'Nice airport. Now tonight we're going to –'

'Forget it, Kev!' cut in Sardine Sid. 'Tonight we're going out – tom catting, high hatting, go-go dancing, disco prancing, rapping, rocking, hip hopping, scene stopping and big bopping. We're going to party till we're pooped!'

'That's what I was about to say,' said Kevin. 'Tonight we'll have a night out on the tiles. So come on everybody. Let's get on down and boogie!'

This is the night out on the tiles that the
Megamogs had.

'Great!' gasped Kevin Catflap. 'Nice night out. Now, I've got an anouncement to make – today, Miss Marbletop comes home. So no dozing, dreaming or dodging. We're going to lay on a reception and it's going to be BIG!'

This is the reception Miss Marbletop came home to.

Then, when she looked
at her house…

This is what Miss Marbletop saw.

And this is what she said:

'Oh my gosh! Oh my goodness!
Oh my sainted aunt! Great Scott!
Good heavens! By George! By jove!
By jingo! Saints preserve us! Oh flip!
Well I never did! Stone the crows!
Blow me down! Who would believe it!
Great balls of fire...'

'I LOVE IT!'

And the Megamogs?

They flew off from the airport
for the holiday of a lifetime.

'Great!' said Kevin Catflap. 'Nice holiday. But tonight I want you all in bed early. No misbehaving, raving or midnight bathing, because tomorrow, we're going to do something.

And guess what.

It's going to be…